Turtlebird's Double Dip Shuffle

by Tara Fass, LMFT

illustrated by
Alexandra Conn

Copyright 2012 by Tara Fass, LMFT and Huqua Press
All rights reserved.

ISBN 978-0-9838120-4-3

First published in 2013 by Huqua Press
A division of Magpye Media/Morling Manor Corp.
Los Angeles, California

Cover and text designed by Alexandra Conn

No part of this book may be reproduced or transmitted in any form
by any means without permission from the author or publisher.

huquapress.com

A portion from the proceeds from the sale of this book will benefit Metivta.
Metivta Center for Contemplative Judaism

Visit the author's website: tarafass.com

Printed in the United States of America

Turtlebird's Double Dip Shuffle
A User's Manual

This book is written for those heartbreaking moments when parent and child alike are converging toward the brink of emotional breakdown. The goal is to turn meltdown tears into smiles. This ditty, Old Mc Donald's Farm meets Humpty Dumpty, is intended to be read out loud and con gusto (even if it seems awkward or embarrassing) because chances are the funny, distracting and attention-getting noises created by the animal sounds will spark curiosity.

Transitions between two parents' homes are known to be rife with opportunities for struggle. *Turtlebird's Double Dip Shuffle* is an arty and light yet bittersweet poem about living the Bifurcated Custody life from the perspective of a child. For me, this was the obvious place to start helping you turn the low moment of a Turtlebird's temper-tantrum to a better place.

As you read, try to identify your own triggers by locating them in your body for signs of your own discomfort. Associate those mixed feelings with the encouraging words the various animals – owls, turkeys, bees and butterflies – have to offer. The hope is this enhances the shared experience between reader and listener.

Your goal is to non-confrontationally jumpstart Turtlebird's edginess to a sense of individual and collective well-being. I know there are no short-cuts to coming to terms with a difficult situation. But in general, by helping children narrate their most vulnerable feelings – by finding the words to match the emotions - the transitional stress moves from distress to smooth sailing. That said some transitional meltdowns are normal and necessary.

Turtlebird's Double Dip Shuffle may help minimize meltdowns but will not eradicate them completely, nor does the book address underlying conflict between parents which feeds the overall tension. Some stress is healthy. It builds resilience. How much is too much is a highly debated issue and outside the scope of this book.

Take this book with you to your custody exchanges in case transitional stress meltdowns start to get the better of all involved. Alternatively, read it to Turtlebirds before bed every night during your separation and/or divorce, for as long as you need it, for as long as it works. Having the animals to identify with makes it easier to identify with the harder feelings in them and potentially in you, too.

If your child isn't a Turtlebird and only has one home, chances are they have family and friends who are? This book will help them understand those children. Moreover, in writing this book my hope is to ready young children as early as infancy and toddlerhood to learn the language of empathy. This book is intended to raise verbal and written literacy through emotional awareness.

Without question separation and divorce is a complex and difficult journey. It's a choice you make for your family and the goal is to make the transition from home to home, parent to parent, the least sorrowful. Turtlebird is a tool to help ease the process for you and for them.

My hope is that *Turtlebird's Double Dip Shuffle* will assist children in the journey to acceptance and peace -and ultimately joy - in their new potentially confusing but loving world. If you're so inclined, please drop me a line via my website: www.TaraFass.com

— Tara Fass

"I don't remember having had any books or other tools designed to help explain and deal with my parent's separation. I think that a book like this is effective because it channels the feelings and thoughts that are in a child's mind without being too clinical. It's not to say that it is negative for these things to be addressed explicitly, but there are many books that do that. This one, through metaphors and rhythm, gives children a chance to react emotionally and express themselves as they read it."

— Alex Linz, actor ("One Fine Day")

To all the Turtlebirds and their parents,
you are never far from my heart or thoughts.

"One day Alice came to a fork in the road and saw a Cheshire Cat in a tree.

"Which road do I take?" she asked.

"Where do you want to go?" was his response.

"I don't know," Alice answered.

"Then," said the Cat, "it doesn't matter."

~ Lewis Carroll, Alice in Wonderland

I'm a turtlebird and I have two homes.
One home a cozy shell.
One home a comfy nest.

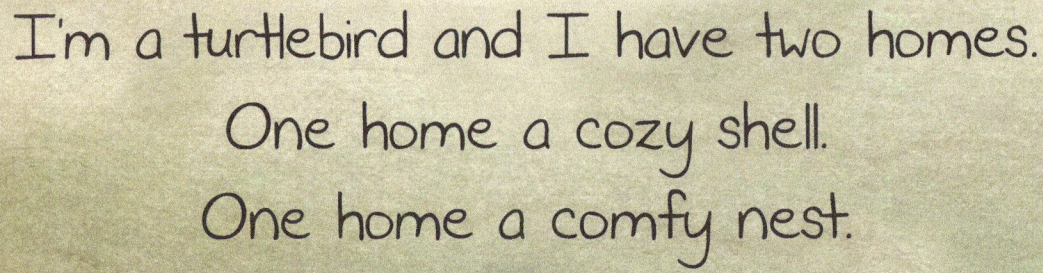

I sleep here. I play there.
I sleep there. I play here.
It's a double dip, double dip shuffle.

Ding-dong.
Time to be with Bird.
I soar up to trees and chirp
"tweet tweet."

Ding-dong.
Time to be with Turtle.
I dive to a log in the water where turtles run free
and splash "pomp pomp."

Bird and Turtle echo

"hello, welcome home" and
"good-bye, time to go."

My special stuff is ready to go.
Owls say "Hoot hoot.

There's nothing wrong
with you.
No one's mad at you.
It's not your fault.

We believe in you."

Bees ever busy, busy, buzz in my ears.
"Even when you leave,
a part of you is always with us."

Big feelings, little feelings
all of them are mine.
Fluttering tummy butterflies whisper.
"Love, love, love.
You're never alone or forgotten."

Happy and sad. Scared and excited.
What are these double dip feelings?

The Double Dip,
Double Dip Shuffle.
It's my special dance.
I'm a turtlebird
and I have two homes.
I'm a turtlebird
and I am loved in both.
I swim. I fly. I'm free. I'm me.

Acknowledgments

Thanks to Huqua Press publisher Judith A. Proffer for having the vision to believe in this title and for knowing its worth.

Heartfelt thanks to mentors: Rabbi Jonathan Omer-Man, Adrienne Levin, Marilyn and Don Rossmore, Perry Oretzky and Lyle Poncher through Metivta for revealing to me how to heal a broken heart and to Leonard Cohen for the soundtrack. Joel Stern for seeing how origami can take a story to greater levels.

To the therapists: Isaac Berman, Janet Johnston, Amy Goldman, Mary Lund, Angus Strachan, Carol Hirshfield, Karin Manger, Deborah Stern and Elaine Bridge, for showing the way from pain to goodness.

George Ferrick, Anne Lintott, Susan Thrall, and David Kuroda, for your guidance helped form me when I worked within the family court system Superior Court of Los Angeles; Jeff Jacobson, Sarah Hoover, Chuck Hurewitz, Ted Fogliani and Lori Ramirez for being counselors at law with insight and commitment to the process; Peter Spelman for being the insider's outsider and Diana Mercer for being the outsider's insider.

Sara Wilson and Ashley Reich, you are so good to me at the Huffington Post and a warm nod to Megan Sayers at Modernmom for giving me a platform.

Thank you to family and friends for your endless readings and performances. You have given me invaluable pointers and reality checks to help shape the narrative: Anne Thompson, Lyn Hamrick, Erika Schmidt, Jana La Brasca, Robin Lerner, Franne Golde, Sharon Rowell, Harris Greenberg, Lewis Perkins, Margaret Rothschild, Deborah Levin and Glenn Harris, Gary Stewart, Lisa Kring, Miriam Jordan, Barbara Moreno, Lisa Johnnson, Deb Baltaxe, Liv Long-Baltaxe and Alex Linz. Michael and Betsy Katz, you helped shape the Turtlebird's dance.

To my parents, Herb and Roz, for giving me life and the original material to be a Turtlebird along with my sister, Tricia, and brothers, David and Colin.

To all of the Turtlebirds who are never far from my heart or mind, let the healing begin.

CPSIA information can be obtained at www.ICGtesting.com
Printed in the USA
LVOW012106280113

317606LV00009B/19/P